W9-BBR-959

The Starveling

By *the same author*

Novels   DARKNESS I LEAVE YOU
DEADLY RECORD

Non-fiction   HOME IS WHERE YOU MAKE IT
THE SEAL SUMMER
MARSHALL HALL
(*in collaboration with Gil Thomas*)

Plays—full length   DEAR MADAM
(*A comedy for women*)
DEAD ERNEST
THE SUGAR BOWL
(*A comedy for women*)
DEADLY RECORD

Plays—one-act   ROCK BOTTOM
NO MAN'S LAND
FESTIVAL NIGHTMARE
THE GODSEND
NOT IN THE CONTRACT
(*A drama for women*)
THE PICNIC ON THE HILL

Nina Warner Hooke

THE
STARVELING

with Drawings by Betty Maxey

The John Day Company
New York

First American Edition 1968

Copyright © 1967 by Nina Warner Hooke

Published in Great Britain under
the title *White Christmas*

Library of Congress Catalogue Card Number: 68-29956

This book is dedicated to the memory of a large gray cat who was my friend and companion for thirteen years

Author's Note

The village in this story is typical of its kind, a world in microcosm where nothing that happens is without impact on the collective conscience. The human characters are a mixture of the real and the fictitious—but the kitten is entirely real.

The Starveling

1.

THE campers had gone. Like Arabs they had folded their tent and stolen silently away in the night.

It was thought that they came from the west country and had probably gone back there. But no one knew anything about them for certain. They were what rural folk call didikois—people who lead a vagrant life but are not true gypsies.

They had arrived in September and taken possession of the bit of flat ground near the pond. Their trailer was towed by a shabby old Vauxhall car. For additional accommodation they pitched a tent alongside it. In the tent slept the two boys. The little girl slept in the trailer with her parents.

The man appeared to have neither craft nor trade but to rely on casual work. He had been taken on at Halsey's farm up the road and it was by Mr. Halsey's permission that he occupied the site near the pond. It was a time when extra help was welcome. After harvest and threshing were over he was put to digging a drainage ditch across one of the pastures. This took him until the end of November, for the land was heavy and he was single-handed. When it was done the farmer paid him off. There was no other work to be had in the neighborhood so after a few days the family moved on. Their going caused little comment and no regret. The woman was a slattern and her children were not encouraged to play with those of the cottagers.

It was from Halsey's farm that the man had brought the striped kitten. It was one of a fluctuating feline population of the yards and sheds and granaries and was about two months old when the man picked it up and asked if he could take it. Assent was readily given. There were too many cats about the place because the Halseys hated having them drowned.

The kitten took gladly to its new life, which was a considerable improvement on the rough precarious existence from which it had come. The campers were kind to it and entertained by its antics. It was much fondled and amply fed. In the bright autumn days it played around the camp, chased leaves and followed the children when they went to gather mushrooms or late blackberries. In the evenings it sat under the table while the family were at supper and at night it slept in the bunk bed beside the little girl. As the days shortened it spent less and less time outdoors and more in the trailer, learning for the first time the delicious luxury of warmth. With the lamp lit and the kerosene stove hissing under the cook pots the trailer was a cozy place. The harsh days of the farmyard receded from the kitten's memory, only to be recalled at times by reminiscent sights and smells—the rumble and stink of a tractor, cow dung on the hill tracks, hens squabbling and scratching.

2.

THE summer had been good and was followed by a
mild dry autumn. The weather did not harden till
the first week of December. Frost came with the turn
of the moon, on the night when the trailer family pulled
out. At dusk they were seen as usual through the uncur-
tained window eating their meal and afterward going
about their accustomed tasks—washing up in a chipped
enamel basin, emptying slops, shaking out bedding. Next
morning they were gone, leaving behind them on the

trampled grass a straw mattress, a heap of empty cans and other rubbish, a debt of one pound five and sixpence for eggs and vegetables from Mr. Trim—and the striped kitten.

Mrs. Mostyn and Mrs. Reece, emerging for an after-breakfast chat over the wall in the fresh morning air, watched as it wandered mewing over the campsite.

"They seemed so fond of it," Mrs. Mostyn said, resting her large bosom on the coping. "The little girl specially. Whatever come over them to go off like that and leave it behind?"

Mrs. Reece detached her gaze from the distant view of her children ambling up the lane to meet the school bus at the crossroad.

"Too mean to feed it, I daresay, now it's half grown."

"Can't be more'n four months."

"Nearer five, I'd guess."

" 'Twouldn't eat much."

"An extry mouth takes filling, even if it's only a cat's," Mrs. Reece stated with authority. "And casual work's not easy come by in the winter."

"Why don't he get a regular job, then? There's plenty going."

"Glory knows."

The two women stared into the morning haze and pondered the mysterious ways of didikois.

Below the terrace of gray stone cottages the ground fell away to the pond beyond which the litter of the campsite besmirched the green.

"Nice mess they've left for someone to clear up," said Mrs. Mostyn.

"Won't be me, that's certain."

"An objeck lesson, that's what it is. Give 'em an inch they take a yard."

"More'n that," snorted Mrs. Reece. "Took my best apron that crafty slut did, or I'm a liar. Anyway it's not been seen since our line blew down. She said she never, but I reckon that's where it went to all right."

"Oh yes, I should reckon that's where it went. Can't keep their thieving hands off anything, that kind can't. Ted's missing his chopper and he swears there's half a gallon of kerosene gone from the drum in our shed."

"The apron our Jinny made for me in school it was, with the pansies on the border," Mrs. Reece was musing.

"The one she got the stiffficate for?"

"Ah, that's right."

"What a shame!"

"Lovely, them pansies was. Every little stitch so neat and clean. Always been clever with her fingers, has our Jinny. A right carry-on we had when that apron couldn't be found. Well, I mean to say, all that work—no wonder the child was upset. She hasn't done a stitch of sewing since. Won't put a button on her drawers."

"Still, she got the stifficate. Now when our Ethel's boy Sam was done out of his carpentry prize—"

"Miss Johnson says," interposed Mrs. Reece quickly, "we're not to force her to it, it's the worst thing you can do. Psychology, that's called."

Mrs. Mostyn nodded sagely. "And there's a lot to it. In our young days the cure for playing up was a clout over the ear, but now they know better. It's true, you can't be too careful. Take young Sam now. His stomach's never been right since that carry-on about the—"

"I reckon our kiddies are lucky to have a teacher like Miss Johnson, who understands about things of that sort," Mrs. Reece cut in again deftly. She had heard the tale of the carpentry prize several times before and it left her unmoved because she did not care for Sam, a sly and sickly little boy. Mrs. Mostyn's Ethel, who lived in South London, was apt to dump him on his granny at holiday times. The Reece children had picked up some nasty ways while playing with Sam. "Mind you, there's been times when I wished she'd take a stick to our Joey, but you got to respect her just the same. It's their minds you got to reach, she says, not their bottoms."

Mrs. Mostyn's attention had strayed. Her gaze was fixed again on the abandoned kitten. Its unusual marking —black tabby rings on a dun ground, white nose and feet—made it conspicuous even from a distance.

"It's a pretty little thing. I'd be tempted to take it in meself if it wasn't for the old dog. He'd never abide it, not at his age, and he gets enough to put up with from Ted." Her eyes swiveled inquiringly to Mrs. Reece, but Mrs. Reece vehemently shook her head.

"No use looking to me," she said. "There's no room in our house for pets, nor food neither."

"It could make do on scraps."

"Not in our house it couldn't. With four growing kids and a man that eats enough for a horse we don't have no scraps. A cockroach 'ud starve to death in my kitchen. It's not as if there was rabbits, you see," she added more kindly. "Time was when a cat could live for a week off a snared rabbit. But them days is gone, more's the pity."

"Ah, there's many as miss the conies. I used to like to watch 'em running races up and down the hill."

"They do say as four rabbits eat as much grass as a sheep."

"Yes, and I've heard it said 'Less rabbits more corn, more corn cheaper bread.' And bread bin going up reg'lar every year since the rabbits went. So I don't take much account of sayings."

They fell silent, watching the fiery rim of the sun begin to penetrate the mist.

"Frost last night," said Mrs. Reece.

"Ah. And more to come, I shouldn't wonder."

"Be a nice day though, when the sun gits through."

Already the sky was stained pink over the hill. Mrs. Mostyn tucked her chilly hands in the cuffs of her cardigan. From a cranny in the wall close beside her a wren suddenly uttered a string of notes so piercing that they made her jump.

"Noisy little scallywag," she said fondly as she went indoors to make up the fire. "I'll fetch him a bit of jam tart. He's that fond of pastry you wouldn't believe."

The kitten, still mewing in bewilderment, had now extended its search to the clump of alders overhanging the pond. In their branches the trailer children had built a platform. From here, unseen, they had fished for minnows with a wire sieve suspended on a string.

The pond, nearly always muddy, was a catchment for the springs and runnels of the hills. It was also the receptacle of awkward objects unwanted by the dwellers in the hamlet. In a wet season when the level was high such deposits were invisible. In a dry one such as the present they obtruded to lend an oddly primeval aspect to the scene. Two old motor tires in juxtaposition to a length of bent pipe simulated the looped coils and snaky head of a marine monster. The rushes that fringed the farther side housed the rusted remains of a lawn mower, its handles presented like the horns of a lurking buffalo.

The kitten climbed up to the platform which, exposed now in the bare branches, was seen to be composed of rotten planks so precariously lodged that only a miracle could have held them together long enough to save the children from a ducking. There was nothing left here to reassure the searcher, no relic of their presence but a jam jar and a shred of blue hair ribbon. After carefully sniffing it over, the kitten clambered down and made for the old straw mattress, now rimed with frost, which smelled of the boys who had slept on it. Here it settled down to await their return, curled up in the middle with its chin on its paws.

The sun rose into a pale blue sky, slowly dissolving the haze and giving an illusion of warmth. Mr. Trim came out of his front door and stood stretching and blinking. Looking into the sun he did not at first observe the empty patch on the green. It was Mrs. Trim who noticed it when she followed him out to refill a kettle at the pump.

"Well, I'm blessed—they've took and gone, Dad!"

"Who you talkin' about?"

"*Them.*"

The campers were always referred to by the personal pronoun, singular or plural, never being accorded the dignity of a name. It was to be assumed that they possessed one, but not even Mr. Mostyn, who was Halsey's stockman, knew precisely what it was. At the farm he was known as Jack, though his wife called him Jerry. The two boys had spasmodically attended school in the village with the Reece children but were in a lower grade and could neither read nor write. Jinny Reece had made some effort to elicit their surname but it sounded like none she had ever heard and she reported that it was foreign.

"Well, dang me," said Mr. Trim. "They must've snook off in the middle of the night. And me owed a bill as long as your arm." He sucked his lips over his gums, for he never put his teeth in till midday, and shook his fist at the spot where the trailer had stood. "There's gratitood for yer. Patched their old kettle for 'em, I did, and mended their old stove, and never took a penny piece. And this is what they done to me, the rotten rumscallions." Forgetting that he was wearing slippers he aimed a vicious kick at the stone doorstop, then yelped and cursed.

"No good takin' on, Dad," said Mrs. Trim placidly. "What's done is done. If you ask me, we're well rid of that lot." She leaned over the wall to rap on Mrs. Mostyn's scullery window. "They've gone, Agnes!"

"I seen that," Mrs. Mostyn shouted back through the geraniums.

"Dad and me never heerd a sound."

"No more did we. Looked out this morning and there they was. Gone."

"Dad's owed twenty-five shillin' for eggs and such. He's proper put out."

"Don't wonder. I reckon he'll never see that back." Mr. Trim was still muttering imprecations in the background.

"Hurt his bunion kicking the doorstop," explained Mrs. Trim. "Never does you no good to let yer temper git the upper hand. I'm always telling him."

"Still, makes you want to let fly, get treated like that. And it's better than kicking the dog, like Ted does when it gets under his big feet."

"Ah. But it hurts more."

"Who'd ever have thought they'd sneak off like that, though? Left their little cat behind, too."

"Left what?"

"That little stripy cat they brought from the farm."

"They never!"

"They did an' all."

Mrs. Trim, shading her shortsighted eyes, peered out over the green. She could just make out a dark blob on the faded ticking of the mattress.

"That it?"

"Ah, that's it."

"Well, there's a nasty thing to go and do."

"Reckoned one of us would give it a home, I daresay."

"Well, I won't," said Mrs. Trim firmly. "Got two cats of me own and I don't want another."

"Amy don't want it neither. What's to become of the creature?"

"It'll run back to the farm, I shouldn't wonder."

"Ah, maybe it will. Best take no notice of it. It'll make off when it gits hungry."

Mrs. Trim went back indoors to wash her father-in-law's Sunday shirt. She had married his son many years ago, after a brief but ardent courtship, when she was a pretty red-haired girl of twenty and had become a widow almost as soon as she became a wife. Peter Trim had been drowned in a rough sea on the third day of their Cornish honeymoon.

His photograph in the policeman's uniform that suited him so well stood in the middle of the mantelpiece between the china dogs, but she scarcely ever looked at it. Nor had she felt her loss very profoundly. Never having had a chance to know her husband, she could not miss him and she was honest enough to say so whenever the subject was mentioned. Old Mr. Trim thought her hard, but he was mistaken. She was not unfeeling but she could not dissemble.

Mrs. Trim proved right. After a day and a night of fruitless search the kitten seemed at last to realize its extremity. The tug of old associations pulled it in the direction of the farm. It went slowly and with extreme reluctance in case the trailer should reappear as unaccountably as it had vanished. Three times, after hovering a little way off, it ran back to be reassured. Finally it seemed to come to a decision. Mrs. Reece saw it trot away up the lane from her parlor window.

"Got that much sense, then," she said to herself. "Farm cats live on short commons, but at least it'll have shelter." She went next door and shouted through the window to Mrs. Mostyn, "It's gone up the road!"

"Best thing it could do," Mrs. Mostyn shouted back. "Hope it'll stay there, poor little creature, now the weather's broken."

It did not, however, for reasons beyond its control.

3.

THE instinct which led the striped kitten back to the barn where it was born did not prepare it to meet a hostile reception. Its dam, the black and white she-cat with the crooked tail, had recently had a litter of five out of which only one was still living. The ginger tom that fathered them had killed and eaten two. Rats had taken another. A fourth, the smallest and feeblest of the litter, she had accidentally lain on and smothered. Now she had decided to move the sole survivor to a place of greater safety. After diligent search she had found an ideal spot in the tractor shed. No foodstuffs were stored here so there was nothing to attract rats or mice, and as a natural consequence the shed was unfrequented by cats. The smell of diesel oil was repugnant but this drawback was offset by the manifest advantages. She chose her moment carefully, waiting till the morning pan of milk was put down outside the dairy and all the other cats were pressing around it. Then she stealthily emerged from the hay barn with a black and white miniature of herself dangling limply from her jaws. Slipping between the wall of the barn and the manure cart, she whisked into the shed and dropped her burden in the farthest and darkest corner behind the oil drums. She was about to lie down and suckle it when she heard a faint mew. The sound came from somewhere close by. She sprang up and ran to the doorway. Standing outside looking at her, mewing a greeting, was a half-grown striped kitten which did not belong to the existing colony at the farm. No maternal tie remained to link it to her. It was a stranger, an intruder and potential danger. She crouched, her eyes narrowed and blazing, a ridge of hair rising along her spine like a lizard's crest.

The kitten had trotted into the yard a few moments before its dam transferred the last of her progeny. It halted and stared around, gaining confidence as recognition of the scene increased. The smells and shapes and sounds were those among which it had passed the first two months of its life. The heavy sweetish odor left by the cows and the steaming tokens of their passage through the yard into the winter pasture beyond, the coughing grunt from the bull pen, rumble of men's voices from the milking shed, hiss and squirt of the hosing, rattle and clank from the dairy and the background whine of a radio—all was familiar to the small animal standing on the concrete and it reacted like a traveler to the sight of home after long absence.

None of the cats jostling around the milk pan in a tangle of tails and whiskers noticed the new arrival, nor did the she-cat as she crept out of the barn toward the tractor shed with her burden. But the striped kitten saw *her*.

If it did not actively recognize her as its dam she was strongly connected in its mind with the other associations which now came flooding back, and it ran after her as far as the doorway of the shed and waited for her to reappear. When she did not immediately do so it announced its presence by mewing.

The next moment it was knocked flat by a spitting avalanche of teeth and talons. Stupefied by the suddenness of the assault and helpless under the weight that pinned it down, it could do no more than squirm and try to protect its throat. Tufts of fur flew up and away. The air was filled with yowls and screeches. The younger cats around the milk pan fled in alarm. The older ones ceased lapping and gave their attention to the spectacle. Over the bars of his pen rose the huge ringed muzzle of the Hereford bull. His dull eyes brightened, he blew out deep breaths and flicked his ears to and fro with interest.

"What the hell's going on?" Mr. Halsey said to Ted Mostyn. Both men went to the door and looked out. Cat fights were common at the farm but they were generally not much more than skirmishes establishing status and territorial rights. Seldom were they attended by the earsplitting din and ferocity of this one.

"Surely that's the kitten Jack Kowalski took home for his kiddies?"

"You're right," Ted Mostyn said. "And he went off and left it behind. That's its mother on top of it. We'd best do summat quick or she'll kill it."

He was holding the dripping nozzle of the hose and he now switched the water full on and directed it at the struggling pair. It had an instant effect. The she-cat ran off. The kitten staggered to its feet and lost no time in

beating a retreat. Still crying in terror and bewilderment
it fled through the gateway and did not stop until it had
put half a mile between itself and the farm. It seemed to
be oblivious to direction, for it ran haphazardly across
lanes and footpaths, over grass and plowland, until finally it came to a halt in the churchyard on the outskirts
of the village.

The bell was ringing. At the church gate stood four
elderly women huddling into their coats against the
sharp wind. They constituted the whole of the regular
congregation at early service. They were talking in low
tones within earshot of the kitten that crouched behind
a tombstone, its heart racing and thumping. One of them
talked through her nose like the trailer woman, Mrs.
Kowalski. For hours the kitten had sat under the table
listening to that voice as it recounted the day's doings,
scolded the children and exchanged banter with their
father. It pricked up its ears at the sound and peered
eagerly around the tombstone. It happened that the
woman was wearing a coat edged with coarse dark fur.
Mrs. Kowalski had possessed a coat with the same kind
of fur on it. The coincidence was enough to make the
kitten forget its fright and fill it with a wild hope. When
the bell stopped ringing and the four women went into

the church it followed them. The verger saw it run in but not in time to prevent it. Now he did not know whether to close the door or to leave it open until he had found the animal and chased it out. The kitten had vanished into one of the rear pews. The rector stood at the altar steps waiting for the door to be closed so that he could begin the service. The verger decided to shut the door and make a discreet search for the intruder. In the event, search proved unnecessary, for the kitten came out of hiding and walked up the aisle. It stopped and sat down beside the pew containing the four women. The one nearest the aisle turned her head and gave a smothered shriek. The kitten presented a sight as deplorable as it was unexpected. Blood trickled from a gash in its cheek, its coat was fouled with farmyard muck.

The rector, confronted with this small apparition in the middle of reciting the Ten Commandments, displayed admirable presence of mind. Without any alteration of tone he inserted after the line, "—and the stranger that is within thy gates—" the two words: "*Remove it.*" Whereupon the verger, creeping up on tiptoe, scooped up the kitten, bore it away and put it out. As it seemed disinclined to go he assisted its departure with the toe of his boot, then shut the door and returned to sit piously in his usual seat, the one under the niche containing the statue of St. Francis.

For the rest of that Sunday morning the kitten wandered about the village. Many people saw it and were distressed by its woebegone appearance. A couple of weekend hikers encountered it in the roadway, stopped to examine it and formed the opinion that it must have been savaged by a dog.

"Poor little thing," said the girl. "Someone ought to do something about it."

She took a sandwich out of her pack, extracted from it a slice of ham and offered this to the kitten who sniffed with interest but did not take it. The drying blood made its face so stiff that it could not eat.

"Well, it's not hungry, anyway," said the man, and they walked on.

In point of fact, the one hazard to which the kitten had not been exposed that morning was attack from a dog. The dogs who might have chased it were habitually kept on chains and the furious barking they set up as soon as it came in sight was sufficient to keep it at a safe distance from them.

While prowling around a council house trash can it narrowly missed being hit by a stone flung by the son of the tenant, and twice it was nearly run over by car-borne churchgoers arriving for the midmorning service.

By the time the worshippers had streamed out and were hastening home to their dinners the kitten had set out to find its way back to the hamlet. Making a wide detour around Halsey's farm it got lost in a kale field, but by lucky chance emerged onto the rough track which Ted Mostyn used as a shortcut in dry weather. In wet weather the track was a running stream, for it drained water off the hill pasture. The kitten followed the scent of the cowman's boots—at first toward the farm. Realizing its mistake, it turned and ran in the opposite direction, reaching the hamlet while the cottagers were sitting down to dinner. Weary and in pain from the wound in its face, it went to the pond to drink. There was an old broken wall around one end of the pond and onto this the kitten climbed. Here it crouched, shivering, trying to clean itself, and here it eventually curled up and slept.

4.

THE cottagers did not notice till next morning that it had returned. Mrs. Reece saw it first. When she opened her door to shake the mats, after Bert had gone bouncing and stuttering up the lane on his old motor-bike, she found it sitting on the step. Gave her quite a turn, she said later.

She pushed the door to hastily. Once let a stray come indoors and you'd never be rid of it. Didn't do to feed it neither, come to that, if you didn't want to keep it.

All the same, couldn't stand by and see it starve. Two days now since the campers went. Drat and *drat* them, thought Mrs. Reece fretfully, why couldn't they take their dratted pet with them—or at least find another home for it, 'stead of turning it loose to pester other people? Just like the didikois. After a few minutes of fuming indecision she filled a pie dish with bread and milk and went out by her back door. She went around the angle of the wall—her cottage was at the north end of the row of three—across the green to the pond and onto the flat ground beyond it. She called "Puss, puss, puss!" and the striped kitten bounded out through the front gate and came flying after her. Having deposited her offering at a point, she hoped, far enough from the cottages to be unidentified with any particular occupant, Mrs. Reece stood back and watched the kitten lapping eagerly. She did not fondle it for fear—as she would have said—of encouraging it. But she stooped and flicked up its tail to take an expert look underneath.

She had noticed its gashed face, on which the blood had now congealed and blackened, and she shrewdly guessed the cause.

"Druv you away, did they? Well now, what's to be done with you, I wonder? Us'll have to put our heads together."

Later that morning Mrs. Reece, Mrs. Mostyn and Mrs. Trim foregathered in Mrs. Trim's kitchen over cocoa and ginger nuts, three stout good-natured women who got on well with each other despite the quarter of a century that separated them in age. Mrs. Mostyn, going on for sixty, was senior by some twelve years to Mrs. Trim. Mrs. Reece was only thirty-four though, like so many heavily built countrywomen, she looked much older.

The hope at first entertained by the other two that Mrs. Trim might be induced to solve the problem of the homeless kitten had been short-lived. She had said again with finality, "I can't afford to keep another and that's flat, not with cod trimmings at tenpence the pound."

It was accepted that the Trims were less "comfortable" than the others. Reece made good money at the quarry now that the price of stone had soared to such unbelievable heights and he had bought his cottage with a legacy many years ago. The Mostyns could live well on a cowman's wage since their cottage was supplied by the farmer and there was free milk and other perquisites from the farm. The Trims paid rent to "the estate," a nebulous concern owning tracts of land in the area. The rent was not very much but at times it took some finding.

Basically the Trims had nothing but their pensions.
These they supplemented in a variety of ways, Maggie
Trim by providing bed and breakfast for the hardier
type of summer visitor, Mr. Trim by doing odd jobs
and selling the produce of his hens, bees and vegetable
plot. Though well over seventy he was as active as a
man of half his age and attributed this to the conserva-
tion of his energy by labor-saving devices. He never, as
he said, took two steps where one would do; never stood
when he could sit and never sat when he could lie down.

His gardening method was simple but effective. Having divided his plot into two strips by a barrier of old
bedsteads and wire netting, he cultivated one half and
used the other as a hen run, reversing the arrangement
annually. He never pulled a weed nor burned a leaf.
Everything was heaped on top of the soil—stalks, weeds,
kitchen refuse, old rags and newspapers—and it all got
turned in at digging time. He made no compost, spread
no manure. There was no need of such backbreaking
practices. He had cunningly erected a scratching post
outside his back gate which abutted on the hill pasture.
The cattle droppings that accumulated around the post
he scraped inside and left for the hens to distribute. The
rich black soil produced over the course of years by such
methods was infested with every pest known to natural

science and still grew extravagant quantities of excellent vegetables.

Actually he did pretty well out of his multifarious activities. Not even his daughter-in-law was aware that he had a tidy sum in the post office savings bank. Had she known it she would have bought many little luxuries she habitually denied herself. The others found it impossible to press her in the matter of the kitten. They had to accept her situation at its face value.

"Besides," she said, "there's Dad's feelings to be considered. He's bitter about the egg bill." If the matter was put to Dad she knew exactly what he would say. He'd say it was hard enough that he should be twenty-five bob to the bad on account of them campers, let alone be asked to harbor their danged cat for 'em. "And you couldn't blame him really," Mrs. Reece and Mrs. Mostyn felt obliged to assent.

"I don't see it starving, not reelly," Mrs. Trim went on. "Not when there's mice and birds to be had. It'll go wild afore long, I shouldn't wonder."

"Be kinder to put it away," was Mrs. Reece's opinion.

"That'd be a proper shame, that would," said Mrs. Mostyn, "for it's a taking little thing. I seldom see a prettier marked little cat. There's bound to be someone 'ud take a fancy to it if they could see it."

"I misdoubt that."

"Why wouldn't they, then?"

"There's one good reason."

There was a pause. Mrs. Reece was given to oracular pronouncements which she needed time to expand.

"It's a *she*, that one is."

"It's never!" Mrs. Mostyn said. "That's a little tommy, if ever I saw one. You can tell by the head."

"Any head looks big on a small body," said Mrs. Trim. " 'Tis the other end you got to look at."

"I looked," said Mrs. Reece. "Now, there's not many'll take a little she-cat. Who wants to be swamped out with kittens? That's why I say it'd be kinder to put it away. Ted would do it," she added, looking at Mrs. Mostyn.

"I daresay he would," said Mrs. Mostyn, "if I was to ask him. But I shan't."

"Nor I won't ask Dad, neither," said Mrs. Trim, "not till we've tried other ways. If Amy's so set on the idea, let her get Bert to do it."

"*Bert?*" Mrs. Reece exclaimed with amused derision. "Not him! He's a proper softie, Bert is, for all his size. Won't kill so much as a beetle."

"That's true. He's a rare one. You don't often see a man as don't want to kill something."

"Well, you two can do what you like. But you better take my word for it, that little cat'll be stone cold dead before anyone offers a home for it once they know it's a she."

Mrs. Trim helped herself to another ginger nut.

"I don't know so much about that, Amy," she said, crunching carefully on account of her top plate. " 'Tisn't like the old days. Vets is cleverer than they used to be, they can doctor a she-cat easy as a tom."

"Yes, only it's more of a operation and it costs more."

"I know what it costs. Our Smokey's a she, don't you forget. Of course, she'd already been done when I got her from the Home. But I know what it cost to do her because the lady told me that took her there—that artist lady that went off to South America, no, South Africa, because her son got in some kind of trouble—and had to leave her four dogs and a cat behind, and a parrot with one eye."

"All right, then. What *did* it cost? Let's have it."

"Thirty shillings, she told me. And she said Smokey was romping around in a few days and caught a mouse."

"That was years ago. It'll be more now, like everything else."

"Still only ten bob for a tommy," Mrs. Reece said succinctly.

"Ah, that's right," sighed Mrs. Mostyn. "Well, I dunno, I'm sure."

No solution was reached. The only point on which three minds were united was the iniquity of the persons responsible for the whole vexing matter.

It was at this stage that a series of squeaks was heard outside and three heads turned to watch a tall figure wheeling a bicycle down the rough path to the lane. Simultaneously another point of agreement presented itself. Whatever happened, whatever was done—if anything was done at all—the person best fitted by circumstances to offer a happy solution to the problem could not even be approached. To adopt a homeless animal was not a thing you could ask of someone with whom you were barely on speaking terms.

5.

OF the two detached cottages in the hamlet, each standing in its walled plot, one was at present unoccupied. It was the holiday cottage of a Bath solicitor by the name of Ferguson and was only used during the summer months and for an occasional weekend in the winter. The other belonged to Miss Coker. Her gaunt figure in its raincoat and stout boots was a familiar sight in the neighborhood, yet little more was known about her now than when she had first come to live there many years ago. She was rumored to be comfortably off. She was a solitary, and reticent. This was counted against her. In a small rural community where gossip is the principal pastime it is considered that anyone who keeps her mouth buttoned up as that one did must be afraid of spilling secrets.

Poor Miss Coker had, in fact, no secret save the tragic and pitiful cause of her presence in the hamlet. She had been one of a close-knit affectionate family living in the London suburb of Blackheath. The house was large and it needed to be, for the Cokers had a wide circle of friends as well as three daughters who were never so happy as when they were all together. Miss Coker, the eldest of the three, was the only plain one and the only one who was unmarried. But she was witty and generous and popular both in her home life and at the office where she worked as secretary to a firm of accountants.

At the age of thirty-eight, to her immeasurable surprise, Miss Coker became engaged to be married. Mr. Collins, a man with a mind as lively and well-stored as her own, was a partner in the firm. They had many shared interests besides their work and were ideally suited to one another.

Since he had no home save his rather comfortless bachelor flat, it was natural that Arthur Collins should be invited that year to spend Christmas week with the Coker family. They were all there—the two married sisters, Alice and Janie, with their husbands and Alice's twin boys.

The year was 1944. This was the first complete family reunion they had had since the war started and they were determined to make the utmost of it. In fact there was more to celebrate than Christmas—even than Mary Coker's engagement. Janie's husband Pat Hagen, a bomber pilot on long leave from the Far East, had come home with three stripes on his sleeve. Beside this handsome figure in the glamorized uniform with its row of medal ribbons John Ettrick, Alice's sailor husband, made a sober contrast. Old Stodge, Alice fondly called him. After half a lifetime in the Merchant Service he was still only Chief Engineer on a small freighter and unlikely to get any higher. This did not depress him, for he was not ambitious. Ettrick was a man who made light of his own hardships but heavy weather of other people's. When the air raids began he worried about his family to such an extent that Alice agreed to send the boys away to the country while she herself moved into the commodious house at Blackheath with her parents and her sisters.

The twins went to a farm in the southwest. They hated it and wrote piteous letters begging to be allowed to come home. Alice would not hear of it; but in the event their exile was destined to last for less than a year. When the night bombing ceased thousands of evacuated children were brought home, the twins among them. They told graphic tales of the rigors of life on a farm— of being roused for breakfast before dawn, of tramping to school through seas of mud and finding all their wants subservient to those of the livestock. The grown-ups listened, winking at each other and clucking their tongues in mock sympathy.

The boys thought Blackheath with its large open spaces a fine place to live in. This was a sentiment with which their grandfather was entirely in agreement. Nothing would induce Mr. Coker to leave his home for a safer area farther from the stricken city. Retiring from a prosperous drapery business a few months before the outbreak of war, he had realized the dream of his life by converting the top floor of the house into a studio workshop. Here he tinkered away at household repairs, wood carving and furniture making, oblivious to the wail of air raid sirens, the racket of aerial warfare and the boom of falling bombs.

His equipment was costly and elaborate. It included

vises and clamps, power drills, a lathe and a small circu-
lar saw. Around the walls were racks holding a shining
array of hand tools of every description.

This workshop was the envy of Arthur Collins who
had similar tastes and hobbies. The two men had known
each other for some time before Arthur became engaged
to Mary Coker.

"I suspect you only proposed to me so you could have
the run of Father's workshop," Mary teased her fiancé.

It was her sense of humor that first endeared her to
him. However black the day, however thick the diffi-
culties under which he labored to keep the business going, she could find something to laugh at. They had a
number of small private jokes that seemed very childish to their colleagues but which caused them much
amusement.

To distract his mind from the ugliness of life in the
war-torn city Arthur Collins spent much of his spare
time studying beautiful things of the past. Inspired by
his enthusiasm, Mary Coker also took an interest in the
subject and accompanied him in his wanderings around
such museums as remained open and the antique shops
that still had goods to display.

He proposed to her in September, 1944, after a flying
bomb had struck a building nearby and demolished their

front office. They had both been standing by their desks. In the terrible moment between the cutting out of the bomb's mechanism overhead and its descent Arthur Collins flung himself across the room onto his secretary and they both fell down on the floor behind her desk. It was not until the repercussions of the blast subsided that he realized he was lying on top of her with his hands on her breast. As he helped her up he was blushing to the roots of his hair.

"I do beg your pardon. Whatever must you think of me? It was quite unintentional."

"Was it?" she said. "How disappointing!"

He stared at her wildly. Their eyes were on a level, the gray and the hazel. Her hair, like his own, was white with plaster. The floor all around was strewn thick with broken glass. Slivers of it glittered in their clothing. She was laughing. He too began to laugh. They fell into each other's arms, shaken with mirth, while the rest of the ceiling came down around them.

"Let's get married, Mary," he gasped.

"Yes, let's do that."

"How soon?"

"As soon as you like."

"At Easter? The war could be over by then."

"Yes, at Easter. It's the right time for a wedding."

He gave her an antique ring, a cameo set in loops and knots of small pearls. The stone was oval, an inch long—plainly intended, Arthur said, for one of the very few hands that could wear it effectively.

It had not occurred to Mary Coker that anyone could admire her hands. They seemed to her too big and bony, like the rest of her. Now she began to take care of them, massaging cream into her long fingers, tapering and painting her nails. She made more use of gesticulation in order to display her beautiful ring.

One night she stood before the mirror in her bedroom and surveyed herself with humorous appraisal.

"Ugly gawk that you are, you thought no man would ever love you. But wonders never cease. You're going on for forty, your hair is mousy, your skin is sallow, your eyes are too small and your mouth too big. Yet inside that unattractive form is a girl who is young and lissome, soft as a peach, the girl that Arthur kisses and who is visible to no eyes but his."

Both she and Arthur, who discussed religion as they discussed everything else with exuberant frankness, were agnostics. They considered that no one who lived in the modern world and possessed a mind worthy of the name could possibly be anything else. But one morning on her way to the office Miss Coker had a sudden impulse to go into the church she passed twice daily. Her mother attended Sunday service here and was among the most useful and devoted of the church's lay helpers. Mary had not been inside it since she was a girl and used to accompany her mother. The time was early December. Already it was certain that both her brothers-in-law would be home for Christmas. The impulse to go into the church was unaccountable—unless it was due to some relic of her mother's simple faith that mental and emotional maturity had never been able to eradicate.

She found herself alone in the bleak and gloomy interior. Kneeling at the altar steps she said aloud: "Whoever and wherever you are, whatever your purpose may be in permitting so much wickedness and waste in a world you are supposed to have created, at least you have been good to me and I am grateful. I thank you for the loving kindness of my parents and for preserving them in good health to enjoy their old age. I thank you for Janie's Pat and for Alice's John and their boys and for giving us this chance to come together at Christmas time. I thank you for Arthur Collins and for the miracle he has wrought in my life. Amen."

Afterward, irrational though she knew it to be, she felt an extraordinary sense of relief, as though she had paid off a long-standing debt.

By the 23rd the whole household was involved in preparations for the big party on Christmas Day.

In default of obtaining a fir tree Mr. Coker had cut down one of the sooty old laurels in the shrubbery. Fixed in a tub ready for Janie to decorate, its scrubbed leaves glossy as satin, it was unexpectedly seen to be beautiful.

All over the house parcels were being hidden away in secret places. Meat, sugar and clothing coupons which had been hoarded up for many weeks were brought out and counted. The morning passed in a bustle of excited activity. In every room of the big Victorian house, from the top floor to the basement, something was going on. Mrs. Coker was mixing the pudding. Alice was making mock marzipan for the cake with soya flour and almond essence. Arthur Collins was helping Mr. Coker to put the finishing touches to a cheese coaster he had made for the festive table. John and the boys were hanging paper chains in the hall. Pat Hagen was doing nothing more useful than supplying a melodious accompaniment to all this industry. He was in the drawing room picking out tunes on the piano and singing R.A.F. versions of "The Colleen Bawn" and "Mother Machree" in a stage-Irish voice.

At midday the handsome bracket clock in the dining

room began to announce the hour with its sweet Westminster chime. Before it ended, a rocket—the last to be fired from occupied Holland before the Christmas lull—struck the house, destroying it and all its occupants.

The reason why Miss Coker did not share the fate of her family and her fiancé was because she was not in the house at the time. A few minutes before the catastrophe she had gone out to look for her mother's cat which, possibly warned by some supranormal instinct, had run away the previous night. She never found the cat and she never forgave it for saving her life.

She lay in the hospital for many months in a serious condition. At one time it was thought that she would never recover. When at long last she was able to leave the hospital she was a changed woman, irritable, morose, shunning humankind.

Having been left well provided for, she gave up the idea of going back to work of some kind and traveled about the south and west of England in search of a dwelling place remote from any town or village. Nothing pleased her. No place was isolated enough. And then one day she recalled how the twins had grumbled about the farm to which they were evacuated during the war. They had written to try to enlist her sympathy and aid.

The Starveling

It's *awful*, Aunt Mary—so lonelie and quiet.
There's nothing for miles but fields and mud. You
can't even see another house!!!! *Please* won't you
purswade Mum to let us come home? We'd rather
have the bombs than the bulls!!!!

She no longer possessed the letter and at first she could
not remember the location of the farm. But by con-
stantly visualizing the childish scrawl, the misspellings
and rows of exclamation marks, she was at last able to
recollect enough of the address to be able to identify
the place. And in this way she came to the hamlet where
she had lived now, alone, for so many years.

The Halseys would have been astonished if they had
known she was related to the two little Londoners who
had come to the farm in 1940. Nice little boys they were
in many ways, but couldn't seem to settle. Always afraid
of the cows, finicky about their food and didn't like the
long walk to school. Mrs. Halsey very often wondered
about the past history of the queer lonely woman who
rode past the farm gates once or twice a week on her
bicycle and never looked in or even stopped to pass the
time of day, who neither paid calls nor received them.

Miss Coker never even spoke to the other cottagers
except to make a complaint. Mrs. Mostyn's radio had

been too loud; the Reece children had thrown stones onto her roof; Mrs. Trim's cats had trespassed in her garden. This last infuriated her. Her grievance against one particular cat had extended till it embraced all cats.

As yet she was not aware of the existence of the deserted kitten—nor, if she had been, would its plight have moved her. No living creature was allowed to disturb her solitude. She lived with the ghosts of those she had loved and lost and with the memories that surrounded them.

The kitten first brought itself to her notice on the fifth day of its ordeal. It was Thursday, a gray and lowering afternoon. She had cycled back from the village and was pushing her machine up the track over the green when she saw a small animal sitting on the path outside the Trims' front door. As she passed, the door opened a few inches and Mr. Trim's craggy red face appeared in the crack.

"Be danged ef it ain't still there!" he shouted.

A missile of some sort—it looked like an old cloth cap —came hurtling out and narrowly missed its target. Then the door slammed with a fearful noise like a thunderclap. But to Miss Coker's surprise the animal, which she now observed to be a small striped cat, did not move.

Continuing to sit there staring patiently at the closed

door, it was watched by other eyes besides Miss Coker's.
From within the cottage, snugly curled in a pile of knit-
ting on the window seat, Mrs. Trim's two cats, a gray
and a black, gazed calmly out at the intruder. They were
growing accustomed to its presence in their domain. The
gray, a female and the dominant one of the couple, no
longer showed resentment by bristling her fur and hissing. On one occasion she had even allowed the kitten to
share the saucer of milk put out nightly by Mr. Trim
for his hedgehog. This winter the hedgehog had hiber-
nated earlier than usual and the milk was being stealthily
consumed by the cats until Mr. Trim caught them at it.

Miss Coker saw the kitten again next morning when
she looked out of the dormer window of her bedroom.
Now it was prowling around the Fergusons' cottage
plainly seeking a way in. She made a mental note to
keep her own doors and windows securely shut.

6.

THE kitten had made several attempts already to get into the empty cottage. This time it unexpectedly succeeded. Two of the ground-floor windows which had been tightly closed on earlier occasions were now open. They had been opened by Mr. Trim in the course of his caretaking duties. He took these very seriously, for the wage he was paid made a welcome addition to his income. Once a week, whatever the weather, he opened up and aired the cottage for precisely two hours.

In the summer he kept the garden tidy, mowing the front lawn, trimming the hedge and scything the long grass and nettles at the back.

Promptly at ten o'clock on this Friday morning he unlocked the front door, went into the living room and opened the windows, thence into the kitchen where he baited and set the mousetrap.

The kitten, watching from the rank grass under the apple trees, heard the casement hinges creak. As soon as the click of the garden gate signaled Mr. Trim's departure it jumped on to the sill and into the living room of the cottage.

The air smelled stuffy and dank. No fire had been lighted since September. The walls, to which layers of wallpaper clung like snails on a stone, were stained with rising damp. The woodwork glistened with moisture.

The kitten crept about with extreme caution. This was the first time it had been inside a house. The vastness, the multiplicity of objects and their strange smells were slightly alarming. After examining everything in the room very thoroughly it gave its attention to the narrow boxed-in staircase rising in one corner to the upper floor. The dust on the haircord carpet made it sneeze but it sniffed at every tread until it was halfway up. Just as it was about to make a daring scurry to the top a loud metallic *snap* sounded from somewhere close at hand. The kitten crouched flat in alarm.

The noise was not repeated but the kitten maintained an attitude of frozen immobility. After a reassuring interval when nothing further happened it went to investigate. The sound had come from the kitchen. The trap set by Mr. Trim had found an early victim. The mouse was a young one, plump and sleek. It sprawled flat under the metal flange which had broken its back, tiny black eyes like beads of jet as yet unclouded, a spot of blood on its mouth. The kitten smelled the blood and was at once reminded of its hunger. It began to paw the mouse, tentatively at first, nervous of the trap; then more wildly as the need became unbearable. It sank its teeth into the hindquarters of the mouse, lifted trap as well and carried it into a recess under the sink. Here, after frantic experiment, it discovered how to hold down the trap while tearing at the mouse. It also ate the piece of cheese impaled on the wire beside the spring.

When nothing was left but the last inextricable morsel the kitten washed its face and paws. It tried to scrub off the crust of blood to ease the stiffness of its face, but the effort was too painful. Wounds heal tardily in cold weather. It leaped onto the drainboard and drank some water from a puddle in the sink. Then it took a short nap; after which it returned to the living room, mounted the stairs and continued to explore the premises. The whole place smelled of mice. The kitten was in one of the bedrooms, investigating a hole in the baseboard, when Mr. Trim returned to shut up the cottage. Being in a hurry he did not look into the kitchen but simply closed the front windows and went straight out again, locking the door behind him and imprisoning the kitten for the whole of that night. It might well have remained there all the ensuing week, living well on a copious supply of fresh meat, had not fate decreed otherwise.

The Fergusons, perturbed by forecasts of bad weather, had decided on a weekend trip to make sure the cottage was stormproof. They had not been down since the summer holiday and, suspecting a crack in the chimney, were anxious to see if this had got any worse. It was their custom when they came down in the winter to notify Mr. Trim and ask him to order the milk and warm the place up by lighting the kitchen stove. But this time the decision had been taken on the spur of the moment. Within an hour or two of forming the plan they were driving south over roads still slippery with frost.

They arrived, bumping over the bone-hard track to

the accompaniment of blasts of the horn, just as Mr.
Trim was sitting down to his favorite meal, a plate of
fat bacon and cabbage greens. His resentment was
extreme.

"I'll keep it hot, Dad," Mrs. Trim said soothingly as
the old man rose, grumbling fiercely, to get the key off
the dresser.

"You do that, girl, you do that." Mr. Trim smacked
on his old cloth cap and stumped out.

Neither of the Fergusons apologized for arriving un-
announced and disturbing him at his dinner. It was not
their way. Mrs. Ferguson, who gave Mr. Trim his or-
ders and paid his wages, was not ungenerous but she was
hard to please. He respected her for this. He himself was
what he described "pernickety in his ways" and had his
own method of doing even the smallest task which he
never varied in any circumstances.

Mrs. Ferguson was a tall blond woman with a loud
voice and peremptory manner. Mr. Ferguson was
smaller, quieter, kindlier. They seemed happy enough
and took a real interest in the life of the countryside,
particularly in birds. The garden of their cottage was a
miniature sanctuary. In the branches of the apple trees
hung nest boxes, feeding tables, coconut shells and vari-

ous wire and plastic containers for food. One of Mr. Trim's winter duties was to keep the containers filled with peanuts, crushed corn, sunflower seeds and other comestibles, of which a plentiful supply was stored in the cottage and much appreciated by colonies of mice.

Barely had Mr. Trim exchanged a word of greeting with Mr. Ferguson, who was doing something to the car, when he was assailed by Mrs. Ferguson from the front garden.

"You've cut back the elder. I've told you before never to cut elder. The berries provide essential food for the birds. Don't do it again."

Following her into the cottage he was further attacked when she saw a strip of peeling wallpaper. "Look at that! I expect you to attend to matters of this kind without being told. There's plenty of paste in the cupboard."

Mr. Trim's stomach was rumbling with emptiness and his feelings were lacerated by injustice. He had made two attempts to stick down that strip of paper but the wall was too wet to hold it. Resisting the temptation to "let fly" he pursed up his mouth, threw the doorkey down on the kitchen table and was in the act of making a dignified withdrawal when the voice hailed him again, this time from upstairs. Mrs. Ferguson had made a shocking discovery.

"There's a cat on my bed!" Had it been a deadly viper the utterance could not have held more horror. "Whose cat is it, and what is it doing here?"

Mr. Trim, halted in mid-flight on the doorstep, shouted back, "What like of a cat?"

"Tabby-colored. White feet."

"Ain't nobody's."

"*What?*"

Mrs. Ferguson descended the stairs shooing the kitten before her. Ears flat, very frightened, it shot out of the front door between Mr. Trim's legs and vanished through a hole in the hedge.

"That's a stray, that is," said Mr. Trim.

"You know perfectly well that I won't have stray cats around the place. If a home can't be found for it you must destroy it. My birds are not to be molested. Your own cats used to be enough of a pest but at least they're now too old and fat to catch any. The kindest thing you can do for a homeless cat is to kill it."

"I don't see fer why. A cat's not like a dog. It'll fend for itself."

"Precisely—and take every bird within range, especially half-tame birds like these. Mr. Ferguson had to shoot that wild tom that lived in the spinney, if you remember. His gun's still here."

"Let him shoot this one, then."

"He doesn't like using a gun on a cat."

"No more don't I."

Mrs. Ferguson, seeing the mutinous set of Mr. Trim's jaw, adopted a softer tone. She knew her man, or thought she did.

"Now, look here. There's a way of settling this matter to everyone's satisfaction. I'll give you five shillings and your bus fare to catch that cat, put it in a box and take it into town to the animal clinic where it can be painlessly put to sleep." Without waiting for his assent she thrust some money into Mr. Trim's hand, gave him a gentle push and shut the door behind him.

Mr. Trim went thoughtfully down the path, tucking the three half crowns into his trouser pocket as he went. He did not mention the matter to his daughter-in-law while eating his belated dinner. This was a thing that required proper thinking out. He devoted the best part of the afternoon to it while ostensibly feeding syrup to his bees. There were three alternatives open to him. He could carry out the order and keep the money. He could keep the money and not carry out the order. Or he could hand the money to Ted Mostyn in the certainty that Mrs. Ferguson's wishes would be obeyed. Ted would likely meet with opposition from his missus, who was softhearted like most women—if he told her anything about it. What Ted would do, most likely, would be to knock the little cat on the head and drown it without letting on to anyone. Mostyn, a man born of generations of countrymen, who had lived and worked with livestock all his life, was not squeamish in such matters. He knew that an animal living wild is often worse off than a tame one with a bad master. There is no master so harsh and merciless as nature, whose laws are inexorable and subject to no redress.

Mostyn had once found a dying sow badger on the edge of a field near the farm. At first he thought she had been poisoned but on looking more closely he saw that she had a terrible tumor in her side that had evidently caused paralysis in her hind legs. Already the crows had pecked out her eyes and rats had gnawed at her hinder parts. He had a stick with him and gave her as quick an end as he could, but she was hard to kill. It took half a dozen blows before she lay completely still. Turning her over he saw that her teats were swollen. This sent him searching in the adjacent patch of woodland and presently he found the burrow with four dead cubs in it. He thought of the agony it had cost her to suckle the cubs until she could crawl to them no longer, and he felt in that moment some of the pain that is the lot of all living things and to which only man is not entirely indifferent. Though he was not what he would have called a thinking man, many thoughts came to him as he stood over the dead animal. *A thing like this—why does it happen? It wouldn't happen to a dog. A man wouldn't let it happen to a dog, even a dog that did him harm. This poor beast she done no one any harm. When she was alive she would've feared me because I'm a man and her enemy. But I wouldn't do what other beasts done to her. And I wouldn't leave her babies to starve like her own kind do.*

It was Mostyn who quietly did away with some of the endless litters of kittens at the farm. Though he said nothing, he privately despised the sentimentalism that denied them an easy death and took no account of the suffering that awaited them in the battle for survival. There were sometimes as many as a dozen full-grown cats about the place and an unknown number of kittens. The she-cats cleverly hid their litters where prowling toms could not find them. Pans of milk were put out and sometimes household scraps, but such provender went to the strongest who needed it least. The vermin

population under modern farming conditions was in-
sufficient to support so many predators. All were thin
and infested wtih worms, ticks and fleas. The worms in
their intestines set up irritations that made them quarrelsome. Some ran off to the woods and lived wild, like the
marauding tom shot by Mr. Ferguson. The deserters
added to the troubles of those that stayed on the farm,
returning at intervals to harass the females and devour
any unguarded young. They terrorized the half-grown
of both sexes. On the whole, however, these rogue cats
were few by comparison with the resident colony,
which confirmed Ted Mostyn in his view that the rigors of a semidomesticated existence were preferable to a
life of freedom. Man, he concluded, for all his thought-
lessness, his gin traps and his guns, was less cruel than
nature. Had he been capable of carrying the conclusion
a stage further, he might have seen the wider implica-
tions of the premise; but then he would not have been
the man he was.

It was not because Mr. Trim lacked confidence in
him that he decided not to delegate to Ted Mostyn the
task enjoined on him. Nor was it due to any sudden
access of compassion for the animal concerned, for the
plain fact was that Mr. Trim had no love for stray cats
and would sooner have seen the kitten dead than alive.

It was not even due to his natural reluctance to part with money since, had he asked Ted Mostyn to take on the job, Ted would have done it cheerfully and efficiently for nothing. No, it was none of these considerations that inclined Mr. Trim to choose the second of his three alternatives. The reason was to be found in the unbridgeable gulf between the Fergusons of this world and the Trims, between the townsman and the countryman. For all that the Fergusons had owned their cottage for a dozen years they were still regarded as invaders. They would never be received into the secret life of the hamlet, never be other than foreigners in a hostile community.

Though he tolerated her high-handed ways and was at pains to give her honest service, Mr. Trim had drawn between Mrs. Ferguson and himself a rigid line at which her mandate ceased. It was in fact the boundary line of her property. Had she ordered the destruction of a creature indigenous to that piece of ground she would, in Mr. Trim's opinion, have been within her rights and he would have carried out the command. It was her bland assumption of authority over matters outside that dominion that offended him. The existence of a stray cat in the hamlet was no more her concern that anyone else's. By the same reasoning Mr. Ferguson had had no right to shoot the old tom, though no one was better pleased than Mr. Trim when he had done so. Many a young chick had been snatched from the Trims' back garden by that cunning raider.

While he worked with his bees Mr. Trim was also working out, though without knowing it, something more than the fate of one small hapless creature. So tangled are the skeins of cause and effect, of action and consequence, that he played unwittingly the role reserved in our theology for God, the planner of destinies. Only a very subtle mind, however, would have perceived it as a possibility at the time, since Mr. Trim had a deep-seated tendency to avoid direct action wherever possible. The upshot of his reflections, the final resolution as to what he was actually going to do after careful consideration of all the factors involved, could be summed up very briefly—could be expressed in fact in a single word. *Nothing*.

The Fergusons did not linger at the cottage. Being reassured that the condition of the chimney had not deteriorated, they left on Sunday afternoon for the comfort of their house in Bath. The car was driven as near as possible to the Trims' cottage and Mrs. Ferguson got out to say goodbye and leave the key with Mr. Trim, who was hoeing his vegetable patch.

The Starveling

"Remember now," she said, after shaking his horny hand, "I'm counting on you."

"More fool you then," muttered Mr. Trim to her receding back.

7.

THE kitten returned to the cottage at dusk that
evening. It tried all the windows, standing on its
hind legs and pawing at the glass. Then it went to sniff
under the front door. The smell of mice percolated
through the gap below the weatherboarding and made
its mouth water. Eventually it gave up trying to get into
the empty cottage and returned to the occupied ones.

It was not yet noticeably thinner, for Mrs. Reece
filled the pie dish with bread and milk and her children

added scraps which they filched from the Trims'
chicken pail.

Jinny said to her mother at supper that Sunday evening, "Why can't we have the kitten, Mum?"

"Because I say so, that's why."

It was not often that Amy Reece snapped at her elder
daughter whom she dearly loved, but she had had a trying day. Her suspicion that she was pregnant again had
been confirmed beyond possibility of doubt. And half a
pailful of soot had fallen down the kitchen chimney and
made a dreadful mess that took hours to clean up. She
had told Bert over and over again that the chimney
wanted sweeping, but it was a job he hated and kept
putting off. The two youngest children had been frac-
tious and quarrelsome. She had slapped them and Bert
had shouted at her. Not a minute all day had she been
able to put her feet up. Now Jinny had started on about
that dratted cat again. She could hardly have chosen a
worse moment.

"It's only small, Mum. It won't eat much."

"Won't always be small, will it? Talk sense. Costs ten
bob a week now to feed a growing cat. Them tinned
foods cost dear."

"I could bring fish heads. The van comes to the village twice a week now."

"I don't want my house forever stinking of boiled fish like next door. Now stop going on about the creature. I've said *no* and that's the end of it. I won't have it in here. Ten to one it isn't house-trained. I've got enough to do without clearing up cat mess."

"I'll clear it up, Mum."

"Will you *stop it*, Jinny?" Her rage was exacerbated when she saw the child's eyes misting with tears. It took a lot to make Jinny cry. "There's nothing to stop you finding a home for it," she said more gently. "You could pass the word around at school. Like as not there'll be someone as knows someone as wants a cat."

Jinny went out of the room without replying. But the idea had taken root in her mind. During recess on Monday morning she talked to Miss Johnson about the kitten and, as she had expected, was given a sympathetic hearing.

Miss Johnson's character and predilections made her a sure ally. She had shocked the appointments board by declaring that it was as important to teach children to love animals as it was to teach them to read and write, and that a knowledge of the laws of nature was likely to be of more value to them in the long run than the study of Bible history, arithmetic and most of the other subjects on the school syllabus.

"Facts can be found in books. That is what libraries are for. Once the mind is trained to ask questions it is simple enough to look up the answers."

She taught that conscience is another name for God and that the worst of sins is cruelty. She said that animals have rights, like humans; and while it has never been proved that they have souls, they are as likely to have them as humans are. She said that people who hurt and kill them for sport are to be despised, not emulated.

Some of these pronouncements, when repeated by the children to their parents, caused trouble. Billy Puckett's father, who worked hard behind a grocery counter all the week and enjoyed nothing so much as a bit of pigeon shooting or badger digging on a Saturday, took great exception to Miss Johnson and complained about her to the rector. Had the school still been under the control of the Church Commissioners who owned the building it is probable that Miss Johnson, with her forthright and modernistic views, would not have held her post for very long. But it had been taken over by the County Education Committee on whom her high qualifications had made a suitable impression.

She introduced some unheard-of innovations, not all of which were successful. She encouraged the children to keep unusual pets and to bring them into school.

Jackdaws, leverets, a ferret, a white rat and a tame fox cub romped and rampaged through the clossroom during nature hour—which naturally was the favorite hour of the week with the pupils but not with the school cleaners.

She was a firm believer in the incentives of free enterprise and competition. Each morning when her pupils assembled they found on the blackboard some such question as: "Pigs are dirty animals. Right or wrong?" "Bryony berries are safe to eat. Yes or no?" Sometimes there was a trick question like: "The Lord tempers the wind to the shorn lamb. True or false?" Each child had a notebook in which the daily answer was written. At the end of term the correct answers were added up and a prize of ten shillings awarded to the winner, the sum being exacted from the losers. Miss Johnson believed that children should learn early in life that personal loss is the penalty for making mistakes and that, though knowledge is worth having for its own sake, the possession of it may bring practical benefits.

Now she sat listening to Jinny Reece with the whole attention she gave to all the small urgent problems her children brought to her. When Jinny had finished she said, "I should like to have a cat myself, but I can't."

"Why can't you?"

"My landlady won't allow it. No pets. That's her rule."

"Not even a budgie?" Jinny was shocked.

"Not even a budgie. Anyway I shouldn't want that. Birds were meant to fly about, not to be shut up in cages."

"It'd learn to talk and be company for you."

"I assure you I have to listen to enough senseless chatter from human beings, let alone from parakeets."

"Well, I think it's a silly rule."

"No, it isn't silly. But even if it were, she has a right to make it. If I choose to live in her house I must keep her rules, just as you must keep mine when you're in school."

"What can we do about the kitten, Miss Johnson? One of us got to do something or it'll die."

"We will give the matter our concentrated attention and see what ideas emerge. Go into the playground and leave me to think."

After pondering for a while Miss Johnson went to the telephone and made three calls. Then she rapped on the window and beckoned Jinny in.

"The pet shop has enough kittens in stock just now. The R.S.P.C.A. clinic has a case of cat flu and is refusing admissions. But we may have drawn lucky at the police station. The sergeant tells me that a white cat wearing a little collar with a bell was picked up dead in the road last week, outside the Stores."

"That's Granny Oddams' cat!"

"Yes, sad to say, it is. They identified it easily. Poor Granny must be grieving and she might be glad to replace it. I shall go to see her this evening and let you know the result tomorrow. I owe her a visit anyway. I haven't seen her for weeks."

Jinny went blithely home that day and told her mother that everything was going to be all right now Miss Johnson had taken a hand. Her faith in her teacher's omnipotence was to prove in this case unfounded, and even though it was not Miss Johnson's fault that she failed, never again did Jinny feel the same unqualified trust in her.

True to her promise, the schoolmistress set out that evening for the cottage at the end of the lane opposite the post office. When she had last seen Granny Oddams the old lady was energetically gardening and feeling, as she said, "fit as a spring chicken" despite her eighty-odd years. But now the garden, previously so neat, wore a neglected look. Curtains were drawn over the front windows. Granny had taken to her bed, her neighbor said.

Miss Johnson climbed up to the small stuffy bedroom. What she saw there did not merely surprise and sadden her, it gave her a lesson in humility. She came from a town in the Midlands. Her knowledge of rural matters was extensive but more of it had been gained from books than from observation and experience. She learned now, gazing down at the shrunken face out of which came an incoherent whisper of greeting, how their closeness to the earth sets countryfolk apart from those bred in cities and is apparent in their living and dying. They do not age so much as ripen, like the fruits of the hedgerow. With the passing of the years they grow and become mellower, ruddier, tougher. But they do not become old till their cycle is achieved. This may be in their sixties, seventies, eighties or even nineties. Then suddenly they shrivel and drop. Some vigorous old cottage dweller may be known to her acquaintances all their lives. They never see any change in her. But one day they find that the change has come. The vigor has gone, the ruddy cheeks have fallen in and they know that earth is about to reclaim her.

It was evident to Miss Johnson that Granny Oddams would never get up again, that she had already forgotten her lost companion and would have no need of another.

She sat by the bed for an hour while the hoarse voice rambled on and then she stooped, kissed the dry bony forehead and went away.

8.

THE kitten had taken up its daily vigil outside the
Mostyns'. It was not seeking food so much as the
sounds and smells and warmth of human dwellings. This
longing for warmth was derived from pleasurable associations and not from physical necessity, for as yet it did
not suffer in this respect. It had a thick coat and was
catching an occasional field mouse to supplement the
food put out. There was heavy frost each night but so
long as the weather held dry and windless the cold did

not matter. Wind and rain are the winter foes of soft-coated creatures. Their fur is a poor defense against either. Dry, it is ruffled and pierced by the wind. Wet, it holds the water and chills the skin. Sleeping in the open becomes a torment. The kitten's bed was the old straw mattress. So long as the rain held off it fared reasonably well. But the spell of frosty bright weather was ending.

The barometer in the Trims' parlor had been falling steadily for twenty-four hours and the elms along the lane had begun to tremble and creak. Starlings stayed close to their roosting places. Whirling gusts whipped up the last of the leaves and flung them petulantly about. Fowls went early to bed. The cottage women fetched in coal and kindling and filled extra pails from the pump to save going out once the storm had broken. Miss Coker made the rounds of her casement windows.

The striped kitten was restless, aware of an acuter need to find shelter. But it had learned the futility of seeking this at the cottages. There was not a shed, out-house or privy whose door was left unlocked at night and into which an intruder might creep. This was due to the deep-rooted fear of tramps which exists in most lonely settlements. There was a derelict hut in the spin-ney on the other side of the lane, but this the kitten feared to enter. The old wild tomcat had lived there and it still stank of this occupation.

The kitten was reluctant to leave the campfire for two reasons. First because the straw mattress and the strewn rubbish were the last relics of its haven, and secondly because from this vantage point it could look across the green to the group of cottages and watch their windows light up at twilight. The eyes of the kitten were as irresistibly held by the chain of lamplit squares in the dusk as a child's by a row of bright beads. The pleasure was short-lived as a rule, for with nightfall the curtains were drawn and it was only when a door opened to let someone in or out, or a curtain hung askew, that a yellow shaft broke the black dark. While there was a chink or glimmer to be seen the kitten watched unblinking.

It stood now irresolute in the rising wind, uncertain whether to go or stay. Finally it settled down in the lee of the broken stone wall. It had chosen wisely, for the wind was blowing from the east and the wall gave what shelter was to be had. But during the night the wind veered to the north and blew with increasing force. When dawn came the hills were blotted out behind a sullen gray blanket whose fringes were drenching diagonals of rain and sleet. By the time full daylight came the ground was soaked and the kitten also. It got up but could scarcely stand against the wind. Half walking, half blown, it made its way over to the campsite to see if there was anything left to eat in the piedish. The dish was no longer there, having been whirled into the pond along with the mattress and the other loose refuse.

The kitten crouched by the spot where the piedish had been and waited for Mrs. Reece to appear. It waited hour after hour in the stinging sleet until it was almost too stiff to move. Then it began to scratch forlornly among the half-buried cans of the rubbish heap and unearthed one that held, miraculously, a crust of meatlike substance around the rim.

Mrs. Reece did not appear that day or the next. Her husband had been taken queer with some form of gastric illness.

He had got up on Tuesday not feeling quite himself but insisting that he was fit enough to go to work. Before midday he was driven home from the quarry by Willie Cobb, one of his mates. Mrs. Reece heard the rumble of the truck coming down the lane. Peering through her rain-lashed window she guessed what had happened and went swiftly into action. First she sent her two youngest children next door to be minded by Mrs. Mostyn. Then she filled both kettles, banked up the stove, rushed upstairs for Bert's nightshirt and put it to warm in front of the fire. Presently Bert, green in the face and doubled up, was helped indoors by his mate, stripped of his wet clothes and put to bed. Willie drove off, promising to call at the farm and telephone the doctor. Soon after Willie left, Bert had his first bout of vomiting.

Mrs. Reece was not sure what was the matter with him. She knew it could not be appendicitis because Bert had lost his appendix in early boyhood. She suspected food poisoning, though what could have caused it was a mystery. Certainly it could not be anything he had eaten at home. But all the quarrymen took lunch packs and sometimes for the sake of variety they shared the contents around.

She stooped over Bert, who was lying back exhausted, and asked, "You been eating one of them meat pies again?"

He gave a feeble nod.

"I thought as much, you silly juggins. I've told you before to leave shop pies alone. The last one made you sick. When you fancy a meat pie I'll make you one that'll be fit to eat. You know where Albie Waters gets those pies from? From the railway cafe, that's where he gets them, on his way to work. Glory knows what's in 'em or how long they been laying around that dirty hole."

"They never hurt Albie," groaned Bert.

"Albie got a stomach like a garbage pail. You got a tetchy stomach, you know that. Oughter have more sense than eat such muck. Now look what you've gone and done," she scolded as she wiped his pallid face. "You gone and poisoned yourself. And serve you right."

The harangue continued unbroken as she ran up and downstairs with pans, towels and hot-water bottles, but the words were lost in the uproar of the storm. The windowpanes rattled as if a giant was trying to break in. Hail drummed on the roof and the wind had the full mad shriek of the norther.

Willie Cobb returned to report that the farm telephone was out of order. The line had been cut by a falling tree. He would have driven on into town to fetch the doctor but the main road was blocked beyond the farm by the tree that had cut the line. Mrs. Reece, however, was no longer worried, for she had diagnosed the ailment.

"You go on back, Willie. I can manage. Bert will be at work again in a couple of days. I shan't let him out till this weather lets up."

Mrs. Trim, popping in for the second time to offer

assistance, was blown halfway down the passage before she could shut the front door behind her.

"Doctor coming, Amy?"

"No. Willie couldn't get through. But I can manage."

"How is he?"

"Sorry for hisself. But he'll do."

"Anything I can do, is there?"

"Yes. Put the kettle on. Make us a cup of tea."

"Wonder you didn't keep Jinny and Joey back from school," Mrs. Trim remarked as she complied.

"I'd a mind to," Mrs. Reece said as she warmed another blanket. "Just hark at that wind. I reckon it's blowing a full gale."

The two older children did not get home till after dusk. They had had to walk some distance farther than usual owing to the roadblock and they were drenched to the skin. By suppertime Joey was sniffling and running a temperature, so he too was bundled off to bed. Next day there were two invalids in the Reeces' cottage. Jinny looked after her brother while Mrs. Reece nursed Bert. Bert had passed the night "in a muck sweat," as he put it, and now felt easier but rather weak.

Mrs. Mostyn kept the two young ones with her. She enjoyed mothering them and putting them to sleep in the big brass bed in the spare room. They looked like two puppies cuddled together in a sea of patchwork.

During the night one of Mr. Trim's hives was knocked over and wrecked and a number of tiles were torn off his roof, leaving a gap through which rain poured onto the upper floor. Ted Mostyn came home after the early milking with a small tarpaulin borrowed from the farm and tried to help him tie it over the hole. But the task proved impossible in the teeth of the gale and Ted himself was almost blown off the ladder, and anyway the ladder was too short.

Mrs. Trim was kept too busy emptying pails of rainwater that day to see much of her neighbor, but Jinny looked in at dinnertime to deliver a progress report on the invalids.

"Dad's sitting up now and Joey's better too." Then she went next door to give the news to Mrs. Mostyn. "Dad's sitting up now and Joey's better too." She added to her little brother and sister who were happily employed mixing a bread pudding, "You're to come back after tea, Mum says."

Neither the postman nor any tradesman could get through to the hamlet, but Ted brought milk and bread for them all. He told how the post office van had come to repair the telephone line but could do little till the councilmen had cleared away the fallen tree, so had to go away again. The councilmen were doing the best they could with everybody nagging at them and they were fed up with the driving rain and the shrieking wind. He said there was a proper carry-on up on the main road and he hoped the milk truck would be able to get through as they were running short of churns at the farm.

In all this commotion it was not surprising that none of the cottagers remembered the striped kitten. They did not remember till yet another day had passed. Then it was Mrs. Trim who volunteered to go and look for it, taking with her some bits of fat bacon and a leftover portion of macaroni and cheese. The norther had not yet blown itself out. The trees still thrashed and groaned and the sleet was turning to snow. Mrs. Trim could not see the kitten, so she put the scraps down in the accustomed place and hurried back to her warm kitchen. Directly she had gone the air above the campsite became alive with wingbeats and strident cries. The severity of the storm had driven a flock of gulls inland from the estuary and they had been circling over the hamlet with the intention of swooping on the hen run at feeding time. After this unexpected feast, instead of moving off to the plowlands around the farm they stayed close in expectation of further booty.

The gulls were a mixed flock banded together like outlaws for spoil. Wheeling and crying, they rode the wind over the tossing trees watching all movement in the hamlet. When Mr. Trim emerged from his back door with the chicken pail he had to fight off a concerted swoop. The sparrows that lived in the ivy were afraid to fly to the windowsills for breakfast crumbs. If they had ventured they would have got nothing. The raiders from the sea were there almost before the window closed. Having snatched the crumbs they would beat on the pane with their hard wings and stare into the room with merciless pale eyes.

9.

MRS. Mostyn was another who looked in vain for the kitten when she was on her way up to the village. Snow was falling lightly and the air was raw but, bad as the weather was, it had to be worse than this for Mrs. Mostyn to forgo her weekly visit to her sister.

Miss Weekes, formerly the postmistress, lived in a tiny cottage adjoining the church hall. Though lamed by arthritis she was one of the busiest women in the vil-

lage, a prominent church worker, member of the paro-
chial church council and treasurer of the Women's
Institute. Every Thursday afternoon barring accident
the sisters met for tea and a gossip.

It was while Mrs. Mostyn was standing on the step
waiting for the door to be opened—it took Miss Weekes
a minute or so to hobble down the passage—that her eye
was caught by the W.I. notice board on the wall outside the hall. It was protected by a glass frame secured
by a padlock. Inside was a printed announcement that
the list of nominations for the new committee was
closed. The rest of the space was bare, and this gave
Mrs. Mostyn the idea which was to cause one of the
rare quarrels between herself and her sister.

While they were at tea she rummaged in her handbag
for a stump of pencil and a piece of paper, wrote out
something and passed it across the table. Miss Weekes
put down her rock cake, took the slip of paper and read:
Home wanted for nice little stray cat. Apply next door.
"What cat's this?" she asked.

"What it says. A stray. Been hanging around us near
a fortnight. Some campers went and left it behind."

Miss Weekes screwed up her eyes reminiscently.

"What's it like?"

"Little stripy cat with white feet."

"There was a cat of that description in church last Sunday."

"*In church?*"

"Yes, at early service. Must have followed us in. Came and sat in the middle of the aisle and gave us quite a start. Looked in a state. I think it had been fighting. Rector was wonderful. Never so much as raised his voice, just carried on while Mr. Timmins threw it out. I haven't seen it in the village since."

"You wouldn't. It's come back down our way."

"Can't any of you take it in?"

"Nobody wants it."

"Can't you get that silly old woman, Miss What's-her-name, to adopt it? Do her good to have something to take her mind off herself."

"Well, of course it would, we all know that. But seeing she never says a word to anyone, won't so much as pass the time of day, who's going to ask her?"

"Get Jinny Reece to do it. She's got a way with her."

"It's out of the question. That old tartar won't have no truck with any of us, nor us with her. Will you put up the notice?"

"I can't do it."

"Why not? You got a key."

"The board is only for notices about the Institute—

same as the church board is for notices about the church. A thing like this, it doesn't belong anywhere."

"Same as the cat, seemingly," Mrs. Mostyn said crossly.

"If you feel badly about it, then adopt it yourself."

"You know I can't. The old dog's that jealous he'd have a fit."

"Well, I'm sorry but I can't help."

"Meaning you won't. You never did like cats since poor old Tinker ate your bloomin' canary."

"There's no need to go into past history."

"I will if I like."

"Not in my house. If you want to quarrel go and do it elsewhere."

"A fat lot of sense that makes!" Mrs. Mostyn snapped. "Anyway, I don't see why you're so tetchy about your daft old notice board. Who's going to fret if you do stick up a notice about a cat? Most people like cats so they'd back you up. It's a good cause."

"Rules are made to be kept."

The affair ended with Mrs. Mostyn banging down her teacup and marching out. Immediately she had done so she was sorry and marched in again to apologize. Miss Weekes accepted the apology and kissed her affectionately, but she still refused to put up the notice.

The Starveling

On her way home Mrs. Mostyn reached the byroad leading to the hamlet simultaneously with the school bus depositing Jinny and Joey Reece. She walked down the lane with them, all three holding their heads low against the driving flurries of snow. The children's wind-stung faces framed in woolen caps looked like rosy apples. They blew white jets of breath, clapped their hands and jigged up and down.

"Coo, isn't it cold!" said Jinny. "Miss Johnson says it's going to be colder still when the wind drops. She telt us to put on two pair of socks tomorrow."

"Miss Johnson got fur boots," piped Joey. "Wisht I had. They aren't real fur," he added hastily.

Miss Johnson had devoted the whole of one nature hour to fur trapping. She told the children that most of the wild fur-bearing animals were caught in traps that were horribly cruel. She said that nobody who knew about these things would ever want to wear a fur coat. Afterward some of the parents wrote notes to say the children had been upset by these disclosures. Miss Johnson replied that she was delighted to hear it, for this was what she had intended.

"I shouldn't be surprised if you got a pair of warm boots for Christmas," Mrs. Mostyn said, safe in the knowledge that this in fact was one of the presents Joey would get.

"Coo! My ears are froze," said Jinny.

The air was indeed so painfully cold that it made the lungs ache and numbed any exposed parts of the body. To distract the children Mrs. Mostyn told them how the striped kitten had gone to church on Sunday. "Seemingly it's turned religious," she said.

Joey yelped with laughter but Jinny looked thoughtful.

"It used to be a custom for folk to take their pets to church, and farm animals too, to be blessed. Miss Johnson told us."

"And a good old custom, too," said Mrs. Mostyn. "There's a tidy few creatures could do with a bit of blessing—that little stray cat for one."

"Now it's been to church perhaps God will help it to find a home," said Joey.

"I misdoubt it. God's got a lot on his hands. He's apt to leave such things for us to deal with."

"Why don't we, then?"

"We're doing our best, love. We're all doing our best."

"Miss Johnson give it out in class on Tuesday about

a stray kitten wanting a home and telt everybody to tell their mums, but nobody's offered for it yet. I suppose it's because it's a she." This was, in point of fact, not the reason. Miss Johnson's love of animals and enthusiasm for nature study had resulted in the acquisition by her pupils of so many unruly pets that their parents were united against her in this matter if in nothing else. They would have no more—not for all the blandishments of their progeny.

"If Miss Johnson can't do it, God'll have to. There's nobody else," Jinny ended glumly.

"Wipe your nose, love," Mrs. Mostyn said to Joey. "Now you two best run on ahead and warm yourselves up. Don't wait for me." The children scampered off, but despite the cold they did not go straight home. First they ran down to the pond to look for the kitten. There was no sign of it.

"I know it was there yesterday," Jinny said. "I saw it when we were going to school. It was setting by the wall waiting for our mum to come and feed it, only she didn't acos of our dad. I wonder wherever it's gone to now?"

"P'raps it's found a place to live," Joey said. "I wisht it could come and live with us. Why won't our mum let it come and live with us? I want a kitty. Why can't we

have the kitty for Christmas? I'd rather have the kitty
than a pair of boots."

"Don't be silly."

"I'm going to ask our mum to give us the kitty for
Christmas."

"You won't get it."

"Why? Why? Why?"

"Because she said not."

"She feeds it, so why won't she let us keep it?"

"I expect she got her reasons," Jinny said sagely.
"Grown-ups always got reasons. You and me can't un-
derstand 'em, that's all."

10.

THE kitten had not been seen for the past twenty-four hours because it had at last found a refuge from the weather. The discovery was due to a combination of circumstances, including a terrible fright.

On the second night of the storm, driven jointly by hunger and inability to find a dry sleeping place, it had gone to hunt for wood mice in the spinney. And there it was surprised by a fox, a thin young vixen as hungry as itself. The vixen hesitated before making her spring.

She had not taken a cat before, though her mate had done so several times since the rabbit warrens were emptied by disease. That moment's uncertainty saved the kitten. It fled like the wind, with the sharp muzzle and slashing jaws very close but gradually falling back as the cottages were neared. Reaching Miss Coker's, the nearest, it leaped onto the garden wall and thence into a crab-apple tree. The vixen waited awhile. Then a sound from one of the cottage bedrooms scared her and she padded away in the direction of Halsey's farm.

The kitten was glad enough to descend. In its weakened state it had difficulty in clinging to the wind-tossed branches. As it jumped down on the wall a shaft of moonlight struck from the storm-wracked sky onto Miss Coker's coal shed a few yards away, revealing, strangely enough, an open doorway. The latch having worked loose, the door had blown open and been wrenched off its hinges by the gale. Now it lay flat on the worn flagstones of the yard. Scarcely believing this stroke of good fortune, the kitten crept inside. Picking a way over the coal heap and between the wheels of Miss Coker's bicycle to the rearmost corner of the shed, it came upon an empty sack smelling of mice and old potatoes. On this it curled for the rest of the night, thankful to escape at last from the torment of the wind and the wet.

It was still there when Miss Coker came to fill her coal scuttle next morning. She was annoyed to find the door wrenched off, but as snow was now falling more quickly she did not stop for further investigation but scooped up some coal and hastened back indoors. She had not seen the kitten lying drowsily in the far corner where little light penetrated.

It stayed there all day sleeping off the effects of its fright.

Awakened next morning by intensified cold, it crept out into a strange white world. The snow was thin in some places and thick in others where the wind had piled it in freakish eddies, but it lay everywhere as far as the eye could see. The outlines of the frozen pond and of the familiar tracks across the green were quite lost. It was a different landscape and the kitten did not know what to make of it at all. The very ground underfoot had undergone some strange transformation. It was yielding, treacherous. The kitten was alarmed, so after a cautious examination it returned to the shed. It had no food that day. Even if hunger had tempted it to venture as far as the green the journey would have been fruitless. The scraps put out had long ago been snatched up by other mouths.

It lay quietly watching the white flakes swirling in the space between the doorway of the shed and the back of the cottage. As the afternoon wore on, it yawned but did not sleep. It was waiting for daylight to fade. For on the previous evening, after finding this unexpected refuge, the kitten had made another marvelous discovery.

Miss Coker's cottage, though it stood apart, faced on the green like the others. All five gateways gave on to the same footpath, and this factor had its advantages in so lonely a place as a source of entertainment. The comings and goings of the residents and of chance callers were visible from every front window. Miss Coker, however, disliked both the sound and sight of her fellows, so she had adapted the interior of her cottage to the requirements of seclusion. What had been the parlor became her kitchen—in which, with only herself to cook for, she spent but little time. The old kitchen at the back she had turned into a comfortable living room. From its two small windows looking onto the hillside she could neither observe nor be observed by anyone. The drawback to the arrangement was that the old kitchen, though spacious, was extremely dark. Miss Coker had remedied this defect. She had had a French door installed in the south wall giving onto her yard, and this served the purpose of a back entrance as well as an extra window. The door, paneled with frosted glass, was not curtained on the inside. Thus, though the interiors of other cottages were illumined only during the time between the lighting of lamps and the drawing of curtains, this door of Miss Coker's shone out every evening till almost midnight. Visible from nowhere save the walled yard, it presented to the occupant of the coal shed its full and glorious aspect, a glowing amber rectangle. The kitten lay basking happily in the delusion that heat as well as radiance emanated from it, stirring up memories of the lamplit trailer.

During the night the wind dropped and the sky cleared. The cottagers wakened to an ice-blue glittering morning—a grand day for a shopping excursion into the town. The frozen snow was firm underfoot. A little party set off soon after breakfast, the children in wool caps pulled down over their ears, sliding and shouting and being scolded for making the path slippery.

Miss Coker heard them go by. "Off to spend their money on the usual rubbish," she said with a sniff.

She often spoke her thoughts aloud, though she tried to curb the habit. She knew its danger.

She herself did not "keep" Christmas. It was her way of revenging herself on God. Her rejection of the festival went so far as switching off her radio every time its approach, or anything connected with it, was mentioned. She did this now, for she had caught the words of an introductory announcement, *"A program of carols from—"* The snap of the switch reminded her that she needed to renew the battery before the holiday period. She put on her mackintosh and boots and went to the shed for her bicycle.

It was then that she found the striped kitten and she angrily shooed it out. It went a little way, then turned and looked at her and mewed. She shouted at it again. So unusual was it for any sound to shatter the monastic silence of Miss Coker's domain that Mr. Reece, who was up and about but not yet well enough to go back to work, came over to see if the old girl was in trouble. When he saw the cause of the outburst he chuckled.

"So that's where it got to, the artful little cuss."

"Who does this animal belong to?" Miss Coker demanded.

"Don't belong to nobody. Bin knocking at all our doors, like, asking someone to take it in."

"Well, *I* won't. And what's more, I won't have it

hanging around here. I don't care for cats. If I did I'd have got one years ago."

"No one's expecting you to *feed* it," Mr. Reece explained patiently. "My missus'll go on doing that. She's not one to see an animal suffer. But 'twouldn't hurt you to let it sleep here while the cold's so bitter. Come the summer I daresay it'll run off to the woods."

"It can run where it likes. I won't have it in my shed."

Mr. Reece pushed back his cap and gave her what he described later as "a sarky look." Then he shifted his gaze pointedly to the gaping entrance of the shed. "Puzzle you to keep it out, seems to me."

He followed this up with a piece of his mind.

"I'd have offered to hang the door for yer seeing it's only five days to Christmas and a time for folks to be neighborly. But I misremembered. I've got other things to do."

He walked off leaving Miss Coker trembling with anger. She tried to pick up the door in order to prop it against the entrance, but it was made of old ship's timbers and was so heavy that she could not lift more than one corner of it.

"Gawd 'elp us, a right old tartar she is," said Bert Reece, recounting this episode to his family when they

returned at the end of the day. "We had a proper ding-
dong. She got no change out of me, though."

"Why don't she like cats? Did she say?" asked Jinny.

"No, she didn't. I reckon she don't like nothing nor
nobody. I reckon she's more'n half batty—or if she ain't
now she soon will be. I heerd her talking to herself and
that's the first sign. One day there'll be a van come to
fetch her away to the 'sylum, you see if there ain't."

"Well, I wish they'd come soon," said his wife. "Be
nice to have someone nice in that cottage 'stead of a daft
old misery as treats us all like dirt. There's few enough
folk around here. Why on earth do we have to git stuck
with someone like her?"

"What's for supper, Mum?" asked Joey, who was
unwrapping the parcels.

"Sausages."

"This ain't sausages."

"No, that's a bit of something special for your dad,
to help him get his strength back."

Mrs. Reece's bout of irritability had passed with ac-
ceptance of the coming year's addition to her family.
Oh well, one more wouldn't make much difference. Be
nice to have a baby in the house again. An afternoon's
shopping in the town had restored her good spirits. She

had brought Bert a piece of rump steak, as much to mark the restoration of her serenity as to provide him with a treat.

"Mum—" said Jinny, who was tipping the vegetables into the rack.

"Yes, love?"

"I've been thinking—"

"Well, that's something!" said her father with a spurt of laughter.

"Don't joke, Dad. I've been thinking about Miss Coker. Miss Johnson says loneliness makes people cranky 'cos it's unnatural for humans. Humans are herd animals and—"

"I'm fed up with that Miss Johnson," Bert bellowed. "If that's what she's been telling yer, she oughter know better. Animals is animals and people is people."

He was still sore about the moleskin waistcoat. Unwilling to set traps himself, he had privily asked Mr. Trim to catch him enough moles to make a waistcoat like the one his father used to wear. Mr. Trim could never keep a secret and the plan reached the ears of Jinny and Joey, who took reprisals against their parent in the only way that seemed open to them. They sent him to Coventry for a week.

"I was *saying*," Jinny continued, "that if somebody

was to *do* something for that old lady, only nobody ever does—"

"Such as what, then?"

"Well, like fr'instance, if Dad had hung the shed door for her. She might be different. She might talk to us sometimes."

"Catch me putting meself out for the silly old faggot after the way she took on at me. Bloody old door can rot afore I'll hang it."

"Yes, but, Dad—"

"That'll do now," said Mrs. Reece.

Joey was giggling. After supper, on the pretext of fetching a bucket of coal and without announcing his intention to his sister, he ran around behind the cottages to Miss Coker's gate. From here he threw a clod of earth at her kitchen window and shouted, "Silly old faggot, silly old faggot!" In the absence of any visible reaction he repeated the phrase, jumping up and down and adding an invention of his own. "Silly old faggot, face like a maggot!" Then he ran away as fast as he could.

Though she gave no sign, Miss Coker had in fact heard him, for she was standing close behind the curtain of her kitchen window mopping up a trickle of condensation on the sill. Joey Reece had a high ringing voice with an echo in it of the voices of her nephews. At the sound her heart turned over with a dreadful thud. She turned and went quickly into the living room and sat down, pressing her clenched hand to her mouth. It was the second time that day that a sound had stabbed through her in this way. While in the village that morning she had passed the builder's yard and heard from within the regular *swoosh* of a smoothing plane. It was the sound that so often came from the top floor of the house in Blackheath and signified that Mr. Coker, shirt-sleeved and ankle deep in shavings, was happily engaged in some strenuous task.

The new smoothing plane had been her last birthday gift to him. He never wanted anything but tools and bits of wood and kept a list from which intending do-nors could make their choice. The boys hunted the common and the bomb sites for him. He was as de-lighted with a knotty lump of elm or beech, out of which he would carve an animal's head with a comic leering eye, as with a rare length of seasoned oak smug-gled out to him by a pal at the timber yard.

On that last birthday Arthur Collins had come to dinner and propounded the idea, jokingly at first but with growing seriousness, that in four years time when he was fifty he should retire from business and that he and Mr. Coker should set up in partnership as restorers of antique furniture. After the war there would be a shortage of fine furniture since so much had been destroyed, and there would also be a shortage of craftsmen who knew how to repair and reproduce it. It seemed to Arthur an admirable idea to combine a fascinating hobby with a means of livelihood. Mr. Coker received it with enthusiasm.

"You'd better look out, Mary," said Mrs. Coker. "For all I've seen of your father since he had that workshop I might just as well not exist. I always say he loves his chisels more than me."

"Any trouble of that sort and I'll sue!" Mary Coker said. She stood up, draped a table napkin over her head, put her glasses on the end of her nose, leaned forward over the table and said in a high rasping voice, "The action, m'lud, is for alienation of affections. The plaintiff is a Mrs. Arthur Collins who married late in life and now feels she might just as well not have bothered. The defendants, whom you see before you, are a set of woodcarving chisels. Their innocent air belies them, m'lud. They are a lot of designing villains who set out to entice this man away from his doting spouse and, I may say, *fully succeeded*, m'lud."

They were all rocking with laughter. Mrs. Coker put

her hand to her side. "Do stop it, girl, you'll have me in stitches."

Miss Coker quickly wheeled her bicycle away from the builder's yard and stopped outside the stores. But the vision and the echoes were still with her. In the plate glass window among the cans of soup and packets of detergent she saw her father's beaming face speckled with sawdust.

A kind of faintness came over her and she leaned heavily over her bicycle.

"Are you all right, miss?" asked the delivery boy coming out with a carton of groceries.

"Yes, of course I am. Perfectly all right," she said, adding sharply: "You forgot my raisins last time. Can't you ever get my order right?"

"Sorry, miss."

"Didn't you check the order against the bill?"

"Yes, miss."

"Don't tell lies. You couldn't have done. It's always the same. Always something forgotten."

"Trust you to find something to moan about," the boy muttered as he went off. "Never miss a trick, you don't."

Miss Coker went home in a rage. While putting her

bicycle away she looked in the rear of the shed and noted with satisfaction that the kitten was not there.

After being ejected it had wandered onto the slope in front of the cottages to sit waiting hopefully for someone to appear with food. Eventually it was Mr. Reece who, in his wife's absence, ostentatiously brought out a basinful of bread soaked in gravy. He did not wait to see the offering consumed, having been sternly ordered not to stay out in the cold.

The kitten had eaten no more than a mouthful before it was set on by the gulls who had now been joined by a company of rooks and jackdaws. Buffeted on all sides, twice knocked off its feet and terrified of the savage pecks that were aimed at its eyes, the kitten ran off to its old haunt under the wall. Here it crouched and watched till the squawking quarreling gang had emptied the basin and flown off. After wandering aimlessly about for the rest of the day it went back to the shed.

It had given up its patient siege of the cottages. After being homeless for a fortnight it seemed content to have found at last a dry sleeping place. More than this. When daylight faded it had something that compensated for hunger, loneliness and cold. It had the desire of its small concentrated being, the jewel that shone for it alone. Hour after hour with its paws tucked under its body it gazed at Miss Coker's golden door.

On two more occasions it tried unsuccessfully to snatch a meal under the vicious attack of winged competitors. After that it ceased to try and did not leave the shed at all.

11.

NEXT morning the Sunday calm of the hamlet was shattered by the arrival of Willie Cobb in the truck. He brought with him Bert's motorbike which had been left at the quarry, a long ladder and some scaffold poles.

The day had been set for a concerted effort to mend the Trims' roof. Maggie Trim, after a week of bucket emptying, had—as she said—gone on strike.

Bert had donated a few tiles from the collapsed roof

of his outhouse, now replaced by corrugated iron. He
and Willie repegged them while Ted Mostyn, at the top
of the ladder, was nailing new battens to the joists. Mr.
Trim, who trusted nobody, wanted to do this part of
the job himself.

"You're too old for this lark." Ted grinned.

"Get on. There ain't more'n ten year atween me and
you."

"Fourteen, I make it."

"Lemme up there."

"No."

"It's my roof."

"And Bert's tiles."

"What be I supposed to do, then? Stand and gawp?"

"No, get out of the way!"

A deal of noise accompanied the task—shouts and
bangs and men's laughter. Bert Reece's laugh was the
loudest and when Miss Coker heard it she bridled and
pursed her lips. She was still smarting from his impudent
rebuke over the cat. Moreover she had seen through
his strategy. Plainly he had intended that frequent sight
of the kitten would ultimately break down her opposition. Thus it would find a home and the consciences of
those whose doors were barred to it would be con-
veniently pacified. No doubt he assumed, like so many

others, that no one lived a solitary life by choice, and
that by foisting on to her a stray animal as lonely as herself he would be doing both parties a kindness. Well, he
assumed wrong. He was not to know, of course, the
fundamental obstacle to the fulfillment of such a plan.
But for a cat she would not be here now, dragging out
her empty and unwanted life.

That evening she discovered that the kitten had returned to her shed. She made no further attempt to drive
it away. This did not mean that her resistance had in any
way lessened. On the contrary, it had hardened as a result of Bert Reece's effrontery and during the next two
days she made a determined effort to dismiss the whole
tiresome matter from her mind. She was both annoyed
and perplexed to find that she could not do so. At frequent intervals while she sat by the fire, her slippered
feet on the hearth, the image of the striped kitten came
between her and the book in her lap. She saw it, as she
had seen it for the last three mornings, lying on the sack
at the back of the shed. She tried again to thrust it from
her mental vision. After all, she had been assured that
it was getting food and now it had shelter as well. Many
a stray was worse off. All the same, there was a disturbing factor somewhere—she could not identify it but
neither could she be rid of it. It was with her now, nag-

ging like a toothache. Something to do with—oh both-
eration, whatever it was couldn't possibly matter. It was
of no importance. She switched on her radio set for the
six o'clock news.

"In many parts of the country fresh snow has fallen,"
said the bland voice of the announcer. *"Road and rail
services are not yet affected and with only one more
shopping day to Christmas the traffic has been heavier
than—"*

Miss Coker switched off. But her hand stayed on the
knob, arrested by a thought that had suddenly come to
her. In this district there had been a further slight fall
of snow forty-eight hours ago but none since. The nagging discomfort at the back of her mind had some con-
nection with this circumstance and the animal in her
shed. Knowing that she would not be able to concentrate
on her book or anything else until she had made a final
effort to disperse the aggravation, she picked up her
reading lamp and went out through the French door
into the yard. After the warmth of her sitting room the
air was so biting that it was hard to breathe. Freezing
again, she thought, as she hurried across the few yards
to the doorway of the shed. Holding the lamp high she
peered into the interior. The creature was still there;
it lay quietly facing the entrance. The wide-open eyes

glowed like emeralds. Miss Coker withdrew, frowning. Swinging the lamp in an arc she looked around the walled yard. Its white carpet was unsullied from corner to corner save for her own heavy prints and the tiny arrow-tracks of birds.

And at last she knew what it was that disturbed her. There were no paw marks. If this animal had gone out to eat the food provided for it during the past two days there would be a double set of tracks between the coal shed and the garden wall. So it had not gone. Presumably it was not hungry. But how could it *not* be hungry? There were no mice in the shed to her knowledge. Formerly there were. They used to eat her carrots and potatoes and even the daffodil bulbs. But as she no longer stored anything edible in the shed the mice had decamped.

She was puzzled about the cat. It looked very thin. It might be ill, of course. In which case, in this bitter cold it would probably not last much longer. The best thing would be to leave it alone in the hope that death would come quickly.

Returning to her sitting room she banked up the fire and warmed her numbed feet. She sat very still, looking down at her hands lying idle in her lap. She no longer tended them and they were rough and red. Her ring finger was bare. The cameo had been wrenched off during the struggle when they were taking her away to the Rest Center.

She possessed no single tangible relic of her home or of the people she had loved. Returning after her long illness to the place where the house had stood, she found the site leveled and cleared. Nothing remained, not even the stump of the pear tree. Every object worth salvaging, every usable piece of timber, had been taken and the debris removed by bulldozers to fill in a crater left by an exploded land mine.

By that time the war had been over for more than a year. The effects of deep traumatic shock are prolonged and they vary with the individual. In Miss Coker periods of normality alternated with attacks of amnesia. Sometimes she could not remember who she was, or where, or how she had got there. At other times, though fully aware of her own identity she did not recognize other people whom she knew well, like Mr. Herriott, the family solicitor who had been indefatigable in his kindness to her, settling her financial affairs and engaging a nurse-companion to care for her until she was able to look after herself.

Her visit to Blackheath was the first occasion on which she had ventured out since she was able to dispense with the services of Miss Bartram. She stood for a long time staring at the empty space, her face betraying no emotion, looking like any other sightseer coolly appraising the ravages of war. Then she made her way, walking with quick long strides, to the church where she had offered up her prayer of thanksgiving. The church was undamaged and looked exactly the same. She went in and spat on the altar cloth. Never again did she set foot in the district. But the memory of that visit was added to others that returned to haunt her. She picked up her book and made a firm effort to read. But it seemed that she had thrust away one memory only to be plagued by another, more recent and more potent. The words she was reading made no sense. She began to fume with annoyance at herself and at the wretched creature that disturbed her peace and would not be rejected. Why hadn't it gone elsewhere? Why does it have to lie there watching, waiting—waiting for what? I will not give in. Why should I? It has no claim on my conscience. Let the nagging go on. I can stand it.

She held out for one more night and one more day.

12.

DURING the night she dreamed that she was taking a tea tray up to the workshop where Arthur and her father were making an enormous piece of furniture, a wardrobe or a cupboard of some kind. While she stood and watched, it grew and grew until it touched the walls on either side, filling the entire room. And still they hammered at it, adding more shelves and doors and whole sections. She begged them to stop but they could not hear what she was saying. The monstrous thing was growing still, pressing against the walls till the walls cracked, bulged, burst outward with a sickening noise like an avalanche. The roof was about to cave in and still the hammering continued, only now it was coming from other implements in other hands, from picks and crowbars and lumps of concrete tumbling and knocking against each other and she was tearing at them with her hands and crying, *"Arthur, Arthur—"* People were pulling her away from the mountain of rubble and she was fighting them with all her strength and sobbing his name and all the other names, over and over, louder and louder.

The cries she was uttering in her sleep, like those of a child in pain, were clearly audible to the kitten. In that icy stillness every sound was magnified. A snapping twig was like a gunshot. Even the rustle of roosting sparrows in the ivy outside the shed reached the occupant within. So also did the patter of claws as a big buck rat ran across the roof.

The rat was one of a foraging party that had traveled inland like the gulls from the frozen margins of the estuary. While going to investigate the ivy it found a hole in the roof. The storm that had ripped a corner off Mr. Trim's roof had dislodged one of the tiles of the shed. The rat slipped stealthily through the opening onto the beams spanning the shed. Here it sat for a moment, nose questing, eyes darting from side to side in the moon-broken dark. Soon it saw the animal lying motionless on the potato sack. The kitten's body temperature was so low that it gave out no scent. Its eyes were open but from that angle invisible to the rat. Concluding that it was dead the rat ran a little way along the beam and was about to jump down and fulfill its principal function when the kitten shifted slightly. The rat paused and squatted. From this point it had a better view of the size of the animal below, which was roughly twice that of itself. It decided to withdraw and fetch the other members of the band, two females and a juvenile who were waiting outside. In a few moments all four were ranged along the beam, their hairless tails twitching, eyes burning like tiny red coals in the half-dark. The buck rat was grinding its long yellow teeth.

Normally this sound would have recalled to the kitten one of the worst terrors of its babyhood. But now it seemed unafraid and lay watching the rats with steadfast calm. The same look can be seen in the eyes of the bayed stag awaiting the knife in its throat, in those of the rabbit just before the talons grip or the fangs drive deep, and of the wounded bird in the reeds that hears the approach of the fowler's dog. It is the look of surrender, of peace after struggle and fear, of recognition of the complementary roles of hunter and hunted, of predator and prey.

The big rat moved forward an inch or so at a time and the others closed up behind. They were now directly overhead and the kitten could smell their fetid breath when a sound from outside disturbed them. *Yik-yik-yik, yik-yik-yik.*

Up the outer wall, over the roof and through the hole, came a pair of stoats which had picked up their trail. Hunting expertly, blunt little noses hard down, they wasted no effort. The rats bunched up together and faced around. The stoats leaped straight at them, taking one of the females by the throat. The buck rat came to her defense but in the absence of room to maneuver the fight became a scrimmage in which the dog stoat was knocked off the beam. It was up again in a flash, but its smaller mate was unable to hold the rat, which broke away followed by the others, and they all went streaming out, pursued and pursuers, the squeaking and *yikkering* diminishing with distance until the silence closed in again.

Throughout the skirmish on the beam the kitten had made no movement. Now it dropped its head on its paws and stared, as before, through the open doorway.

The moon waned. Just before dawn a line of swans flew past. *Honk-ahonk* they sang, high in the blanching sky.

Day came, and slowly passed.

Shortly before her suppertime on Christmas Eve Miss Coker suddenly rose from her chair, took the lamp and went out to the shed. The kitten lay as before, its eyes fixed on the golden rectangle framed in the dark. It stirred as she approached, lifting its head. She stooped and with an abrupt movement passed her hand over its body. It was the first time in nearly twenty years that she had allowed herself to fondle a living creature, animal or human, lest this too should be taken from her. The touch of the soft fur caused something to happen inside her, some easing of the frozen heart. The kitten struggled to its feet, arching itself under her hand. The white parts of its coat were soiled with coal dust. She understood then that it was too weak to clean itself, let alone go in search of food.

She straightened her back and went indoors again. She set two saucers side by side on her kitchen floor. One she filled with warm milk. In the other she put, chopped small, a slice of raw liver which represented half the meal she had planned to cook for herself. From the cupboard under the stairs she took a square shallow box which had once held apples. Lining it with an old knitted shawl, she put this improvised basket down near the fire. Then she threw wide the glass door and spoke one word.

"Come—"

The kitten had followed her a little way when she left the shed. Now it crouched in the snow a few yards from where she stood. Its tail was flattened, its eyes unnaturally big in the starved face. It stole forward a few steps into the fringe of the pool of light. A few more, then a tottering run took it to the threshold where it paused uncertain, hovering between hope and disbelief. Miss Coker stooped and picked it up.

It lay passive, pushing its bony little skull against her chin. Light as a bird it seemed. The draggled fur under her hand was not only without warmth but without resilience, more like the coat of a dead creature than a live one.

The feeble heartbeats of the little body emphasized the strength of her own. Standing there alone in the ice-bound hush of the dying year, she was suddenly and deeply aware of this pulsing beat within her. Words came into her head, in the voice of an old silver-haired man reading the lesson in church while she was sitting beside her mother, a tall schoolgirl in a brown blazer and pleated skirt.

"I am the Resurrection and the Life—"

Then, just as it had been all those years ago, a burst of childish voices broke the stillness. They belonged so aptly to that scene of the distant past that they were difficult to detach from it. Yet Miss Coker knew, when her memory jerked back again to the present, that they were real. They were still going on and they sounded very close at hand. The Reece children were singing carols outside her gate.

"We three kings of Orien-tar—" Their reedy altos soared and dipped. Behind them, faint but sweet, came a far-off chime of church bells.

Miss Coker listened intently for a long moment before turning back into the firelit room. The golden door closed softly behind her as the kitten rode into its haven on her breast.

47

Hooke
The starveling

X